RACING STRIPES

A Junior Novelization

Adapted by
David Schmidt

from his screenplay

TM

Scholastic Inc.

New York   Toronto   London   Auckland   Sydney
Mexico City   New Delhi   Hong Kong   Buenos Aires

No part of this publication may be reproduced in whole or in part, or stored in a retrieval system, or transmitted in any form or by any means, electronic, mechanical, photocopying, recording, or otherwise, without written permission of the publisher. For information regarding permission, write to Scholastic Inc., Attention: Permissions Department, 557 Broadway, New York, NY 10012.

ISBN 0-439-71875-9

Designed by Rick DeMonico
12 11 10 9 8 7 6 5 4 3 2 1   5 6 7 8 9/0
Printed in the U.S.A.
First printing, January 2005

Contents

1 Out of the Box   1

2 New Friends   6

3 Blue Moon Races   16

4 The "Hit" Pelican   27

5 On Zebraback   38

6 Lunch for a Lion   49

7 Memories and Dreams   58

8 Paying the Price   67

9 Break for Freedom   77

10 Post Time   86

11 Racing Stripes   90

12 Heart of a Champion   94

13 The Winner   98

RACING STRIPES

CHAPTER

Out of the Box

Lightning split the sky, illuminating a small, broken-down circus wagon at the side of a country road. Black and white stripes covered the entire wagon. It was the last of many vehicles in a long procession. The circus animals wailed and brayed and trumpeted and roared, fearfully. They didn't like being stopped in the storm.

The circus boss got out of the lead truck and walked back to the broken-down wagon. "What's taking so long?" he called to the driver.

"We're having trouble fixing the flat," the driver replied. "Wagon's too heavy for the jack." He pointed to the back, where three circus performers were trying to manhandle a tire onto the aging vehicle. The "new" tire was nearly as beat up as the old one.

"We took out all the animals to lighten the load, but . . ." he shrugged. "She's an old truck, boss. Ain't easy to work on. Don't worry, though, we're almost done."

"Better be," the circus boss said. "We're behind schedule. Can't afford to wait for stragglers."

The driver nodded. He rushed to help the others with the flat as the storm intensified.

By the time the new tire was changed, the pouring rain had made it impossible to see more than a few feet in any direction. The performers quickly reloaded the animal boxes onto their wagon, then piled inside and drove away. In their haste, no one noticed the single, small animal crate left behind by the side of the road. And no one heard the frightened bray of the creature inside the forgotten box.

A baby zebra poked his head out just in time to see the last truck disappear over a hill. He craned his neck, trying to find his parents. Their boxes had been nearby just a moment ago. Now he was by himself, alone in the dark, freezing rain.

The baby zebra was very wet, very cold, and very, very afraid.

A huge lightning flash lit up the sky, and the zebra could see a road sign that read: NOW ENTERING BOONE

COUNTY, HOME OF THE KENTUCKY OPEN. But as the baby zebra couldn't read, he had no idea where he was.

"BAH-WRONK!" he brayed. "Mommy! Daddy! Come get me!"

It was no use. The storm swallowed his cries for help. The fragile, newborn hunkered down in his box, shivering violently. He needed a miracle.

After what seemed like forever, a light suddenly appeared around the corner of the road. The zebra looked up just in time to see a huge shape barreling toward him. It had bright round eyes. It was bigger than a hippo and it rumbled like an angry lion. The startled baby zebra didn't even have time to cry out.

The metal monster let out a screeching wail, then stopped just inches short of the zebra's crate. The baby zebra now saw that this wasn't another animal, it was a metal wagon. It was similar to the circus wagons he had known, but smaller. Had the circus people come back for him?

Nolan Walsh, a kind-faced, middle-aged man, hopped out of his rusty farm truck, amazed at what he saw.

"Hey, there . . . are you all right?" he asked as he walked cautiously toward the baby zebra's box.

"BAH-WRONK!" the zebra brayed.

"What in the world are you doing out here?" Nolan wondered. He gazed up at the rain-filled sky. "Well, I certainly can't leave you here."

He wrapped his strong arms around the crate and lifted it. "Let's get you home and dry you off."

Nolan put the baby zebra in the back of his truck and drove to the Walsh farm. The farm was old and almost as run-down as the truck, but it was home, and he loved it with all his heart.

Nolan honked the truck's horn to announce his arrival. Then he pulled into the barn and unloaded the box.

Channing Walsh, thirteen years old and full of tomboy enthusiasm, dashed into the barn. "Wow!" she blurted. "Can we keep him, Daddy?"

"We can't take care of him properly," Nolan replied. "We should call a zoo and . . ."

"Dad! They'll put him in a cage!" Channing shot back. "No zoos! Come on, you've worked with horses your whole life. He's no different. We can take care of him. I know we can."

Nolan rubbed his chin thoughtfully. "We'll see," he said. "But first, we need to get him some blankets and warm milk."

Channing bolted out of the barn to get the supplies. Her dad followed slowly, deep in thought. He hadn't seen his daughter this happy in a long, long time. Maybe having this baby zebra on the farm wasn't such a crazy idea after all. . . .

CHAPTER

New Friends

The zebra craned his neck out of the box, looking around. His crate sat under a bare light bulb that dangled from the barn's ceiling. The rest of the barn was dark. Strange animal smells drifted to his black nose. All sorts of thoughts raced through his mind. Had the new people abandoned him, too? Were there lions hiding in the darkness, waiting to pounce on him?

"Ever seen like anything like it, Tucker?" said a strong voice from the gloom.

"What's to see?" a grouchy voice grumbled back. "You seen one funny-lookin' horse, you seen 'em all."

The zebra wanted to run from the strange voices, but he couldn't get out of his box. And just then, the owners of the voices stepped into the light.

Franny, a wise old goat, led the way. Her mostly

white coat had a few streaks of gray running through it. Tucker, a dark brown Shetland Pony with a bad disposition, followed closely behind. And Reggie, the dumbest Rhode Island Red rooster who ever lived, brought up the rear. They circled the crate and studied this strange-looking newcomer.

Tucker finally broke the silence. "The kid ain't from around here, that's for sure," he said.

Reggie squawked loudly, "Well, subdivide me and Kentucky-fry me!" He turned to Tucker. "You know, you cut the bangs off, you guys kinda look like cousins."

Tucker looked at Reggie and cleared his throat.

"Just thinking out loud! Thinking out loud," Reggie chattered before Tucker could say anything.

Franny approached the zebra colt. Question time. "What *are* you, little guy?" she asked kindly.

"I . . . I don't know," the zebra replied, his voice quivering.

"Okay, we can rule out 'genius,'" Tucker said.

Franny shot him a dirty look. "Don't make me chew open a can of pony whup," she said.

"Save the sweet talk for later," Tucker replied.

"Maybe he's one of those armadillos," Reggie guessed.

"Shut your feed hole," Tucker snapped at him.

"Pay no attention to him," Franny said. She turned to the little zebra. "He's all whinny, and no bite. I'm Franny. This is Reggie the Rooster, and Mr. Sensitive here is Tucker."

"Hey! Lay off me, old goat," Tucker said.

The sound of human footsteps echoed from outside the barn.

"It's the chief!" Tucker whispered. Tucker, Franny, and Reggie quickly disappeared back into the shadows. The zebra could still hear them arguing.

"You used to be so nice," Franny said.

"Yeah, I know," Tucker replied. "But I got over it."

"Wait, don't go!" the zebra bawled. "BAH-WRONK!"

Nolan and Channing Walsh had come back carrying blankets and a baby bottle full of warm milk. Nolan carefully lifted the young zebra out of his crate and set him down on the barn floor. "He's going to have strong legs. He's quite a little athlete," Nolan said. "Channing, see if he'll come to you."

Channing nodded eagerly and backed up a few paces. "Come here, boy. Come on!"

The zebra looked at Channing shyly. She seemed like a nice girl, but he was still scared and wet and cold.

"Hey, buddy," Channing said, "are you hungry?" She held the bottle of milk out to him.

The zebra wobbled forward, his legs unsteady. He gazed wonderingly at the girl.

"You know," Channing said, "drink?" She held the bottle to her mouth and pretended to take a drink. Some of the milk squirted onto her cheek.

The zebra took another step toward Channing, then licked the milk off her cheek. She hugged him, then helped him drink from the bottle. "Atta boy," she said. "Welcome to your new home, Stripes."

"Stripes?" her dad asked.

"What else would we call him . . . Spot?" Channing joked. She turned to the zebra. "You like that name, don't you? *Stripes*." Stripes let out a loud burping response. Channing and her dad burst out laughing.

"I'll take that as a yes," Nolan said.

Three months passed quickly. Channing and Stripes quickly became friends as the little zebra grew accustomed to life on the farm. They chased each other around the yard, playing tag. They tried to get Lightning, the farm dog, to join them, but he was much too slow and lazy.

Channing treated Stripes as though he were like any other horse. So he figured that's what he was — a strangely colored horse. And the other animals on the farm soon warmed up to the sweet, cheerful young animal in their midst — even grouchy old Tucker.

"Hey, slow down! Boy oh boy, kids these days. No control. Back in my day —" Tucker neighed at the zebra.

"Oh, here we go again with the ancient history lesson," Franny teased. "Enough!"

Stripes raced toward Lookout Hill, the highest piece of land on the Walsh farm. He loved to run, whether with Channing (who was getting far too slow to keep up with him) or with the other animals.

As Stripes neared the top of the hill, he heard a distant trumpet echo through the valley. The little zebra stopped dead in his tracks and stared down at a huge, flat oval in the valley below. A big building, with many seats for holding people, stood nearby. People in colorful clothing were filling up the stands.

As Stripes watched, a row of horses trotted onto the dirt oval. It all looked very exciting.

Tucker and Franny huffed and puffed as they finally caught up to Stripes. "Now we're in for it!" mumbled Tucker.

"Wow! What's that?" Stripes asked Tucker.

"That's the racetrack, kid. It's the only reason for a horse to live."

"There's more to life than running around in a circle!" Franny retorted.

"Well, maybe to you," Tucker said. "It's like this. There's a human race. And there are horse races. And there's even a Chicken Run. But it's funny, I don't think there's ever been a goat race. Ever. So I don't think you'd understand."

"I want to race!" Stripes said. "Can I race?"

"It's complicated. You can't just show up and start racing," Tucker replied. "You have to train. It takes a lot of work to become a racehorse."

"What's a racehorse?" Stripes asked.

"What's a racehorse? They're the greatest. Once a year, there's a big race to see who's the best of the best. The horses that we trained used to win it every year," Tucker said.

"Why did you quit?" Stripes asked.

Tucker and Franny glanced at each other, then lowered their eyes.

"A few years ago," Franny explained, "the little girl's mother had a horrible accident. She was a rider. She fell off a horse."

Tucker shook his head. "It wasn't her fault," he added. "Her horse stumbled. And they couldn't save her."

"Did she . . . die?" Stripes asked.

Both the pony and goat nodded sadly.

"The little girl's father — the Chief — couldn't bear to train another racehorse after that," Franny added.

Tucker blinked away some moisture from the corner of his eye. He wasn't really as mean or tough as he acted. "Hey, look!" he said. "They're ready to go."

The zebra, the pony, and the goat watched as the jockeys led their horses into the starting gate. A loud bell sounded, and the horses leapt from the gate and streaked around the dirt oval.

"How come none of them have stripes?" Stripes asked.

Franny and Tucker glanced at each other. "Aaah, just unlucky, I guess," Tucker said.

"Look at 'em!" Stripes exclaimed. He was mesmerized. "Look at 'em run!" He began to run around the hilltop, imitating the horses below.

"Well, would you look at him!" Franny said to Tucker. "He loves to run. It's in his heart."

Tucker frowned. "Yeah, but that's not enough."

"You could train him. Then it would be enough," Franny whispered.

The old pony shook his head. "His legs are too short, his head's too big, and he's funny-looking to boot. He's got as much of a chance to race as I do. Besides, I've got better things to do."

"Oh, go fix your hair," Franny snapped.

"I heard that!" Tucker said.

But Stripes hadn't heard Tucker's gloomy assessment. He sprinted toward the fence that ran around the Walsh farm never taking his eyes off the racetrack. As he ran, he let out his distinctive bray:

"BAH-WRONK!"

On the other side of the fence was the Dalrymple estate, one of the most lavish horse-training facilities in the world. The estate's owner, Clara Dalrymple, raised her horses to be professional racers. Carla's horses had the best of everything that money could buy. For years, Nolan had worked as Clara's head trainer.

Trenton's Pride and Ruffshod, two young, strong

colts, were used to having attention lavished on them. Everything they wanted, they got, just like the rest of the horses from the Dalrymple estate. When they saw Stripes, they were curious, so they approached the fence line.

"Whoa. Nice mohawk!" Pride laughed.

"You guys training to race?" Stripes asked them from the other side of the fence.

The two colts nodded, and the three of them raced across the countryside, separated only by the fence between the two properties.

Joy filled Stripes' heart. *This must be how it feels to race on the big track,* he thought.

A sudden, loud neigh split the air. Pride and Ruffshod stopped.

"Dude, it's your dad," Ruffshod said.

"Great," Pride sighed. They ran off to meet a tall bay stallion waiting near the Dalrymple stables.

Stripes pulled up, confused.

Tucker trotted up beside the zebra as Stripes watched the big bay stallion give his new friends a stern lecture.

"Who's that?" Stripes asked Tucker.

"That's Sir Trenton," the pony replied. "The winningest racehorse ever."

"He won the big race?" Stripes asked.

"More than once," Tucker confirmed. "He's the leader over there. That was his son you were talking to, Trenton's Pride. The other horse, the one who's always following him around, is Ruffshod."

Sir Trenton glared at Stripes, then turned and walked away. Trenton's Pride and Ruffshod followed.

"Why won't they play with me anymore?" Stripes asked.

"Don't worry about it. You're just different. That's all," said Tucker.

Stripes looked at Tucker in confusion.

"You don't look like them, kid, so they think they're better than you," Tucker explained.

"That's pretty silly," Stripes said.

"Yeah," Tucker replied. "But that's just how some horses are. For some horses, different is scary."

"But Trenton's Pride doesn't have to be like his dad," Stripes said.

Tucker just shook his head. "Kid, it's hard to fight what you were born into."

CHAPTER

Blue Moon Races

Years seemed to pass with the swiftness of a Kentucky horse race. Stripes grew stronger and faster. He waited by the mailbox every day and raced the crazy mailman and his mail truck down the fence line. And he played tag with Channing every day, too. He was way too fast for her to keep up with now, but Stripes loved Channing, so once in a while he'd slow down and let her catch him. Channing was growing up, too. She was sixteen now — almost a grown woman.

One morning, after chasing the mail truck, Stripes decided to run along the fence between the Walsh farm and the Dalrymple estate. On the other side of the fence, Clara Dalrymple stood and watched a young filly work out in a nearby training ring.

When the filly missed a jump over one of the low fences, Clara stormed over to the filly's rider. He cowered as she approached. Everyone in Boone county was afraid of Clara Dalrymple — everyone that is, except Nolan Walsh.

When Clara was done yelling at the rider, the little filly headed toward Lookout Hill, where Ruffshod and Trenton's Pride were grazing.

Stripes had never seen a filly before. He ran toward the hill as fast as he could and bumped right into a tree on the way.

"Yo, yo, yo, Pride, check out the new filly!" Ruffshod called. "What a mane!"

Pride chimed in. "Wow, look at those flanks!"

"Watch," Ruffshod said, "she's gonna come straight for me." He bared his teeth at Pride. "Do I have anything in my teeth?"

Pride sighed. "You always have something in your teeth, Ruffshod." He called out to the filly. "Excuse me! Would you care to join me for a drink?"

For a moment, it looked like the filly might stop and talk with Pride and Ruffshod, but she ran right past them. "Uh, no" she replied. "Talk to the tail, boys." She stopped near the fence line to graze, and Stripes skidded up next to her.

The filly smiled. "Did you ever consider going around that tree instead of running through it?"

"Yeah," Stripes replied playfully, "it usually moves out of my way."

"I've never heard of a tree doing that!" the filly said, laughing.

"You just don't know the trees around here," said Stripes. "Are you new?"

"I just got here," she replied. "I'm Sandy."

"I'm Stripes."

She tilted her head and looked at him sideways. "You don't say," she said.

As she shifted ever so slightly, the morning sun reflected off her pure white coat, making it glisten from head to hoof. Stripes felt funny inside. She was the most beautiful thing he had ever seen.

"Are you a racer?" Stripes asked.

"I'm a jumper," Sandy replied. "I've actually competed around the world."

Feeling full of nervous energy, Stripes ran circles on his side of the fence. "I'm a racer," he said. "I've raced around . . . well, around here, mostly. I'm training to be in the big race."

Sandy smiled. "By racing the mailman?"

Stripes shook his head, and his bristly mane stood

up. "The other horses don't want to race me — I'm just way too fast for them."

At that moment, Trenton's Pride and Ruffshod cantered up to the fence.

"He's no racer," Pride scoffed. Sir Trenton's son had grown strong and fast in the last three years. His head towered above the fence — and over Stripes' head, too.

Ruffshod had grown as well, into a huge brute of a horse. He sneered at Stripes. "They say his dad's a horse and his mom's a fence," he added.

Sandy scowled at Ruffshod. "Oh, real funny. I've gotta go. I'll see you around, Stripes."

As Sandy trotted off, Trenton's Pride showed his teeth to Stripes, though you couldn't exactly call his expression a smile. "Still racing the mailman, Stripey?" he asked sarcastically.

"Oh, the mailman wasn't racing him," said Ruffshod. "He was running away from him!"

Stripes glared back at him. The three of them hadn't gotten along since that first day at the fence. Stripes often wondered what Sir Trenton had said to his son that day — though he supposed it didn't really matter. From then on, Trenton's Pride and Ruffshod had gone out of their way to make fun of him.

"I'll race you any time you want," Stripes told Trenton's Pride.

The huge horse looked down his nose at the zebra. "Well, unfortunately, I don't race nobodies," he said.

"Yeah!" Ruffshod chimed in.

"Figures," Stripes said, shrugging. "All talk and no action."

Out of nowhere, a huge shadow fell between the zebra and the young stallion. Both of them looked up and saw the massive form of Sir Trenton towering over them.

"Listen, you," he said to Stripes, "I want you to stop bothering my son. And you can tell Tucker I said that. Trenton's Pride is a champion with a real future, and you . . . well, you have your place."

"Mr. Sir Trenton, sir," Ruffshod put in. "We've been trying to get this guy to stop bothering us, but he just won't stop . . ."

"Ruffshod," Pride whispered, trying to get his friend to stop talking.

". . . bothering us," Ruffshod finished.

Sir Trenton stared coldly at the other horse. "Shut up, you idiot!" he snapped. Then he turned and headed downhill.

"Yes, Mr. Sir Trenton, sir!" Ruffshod replied. "And may I say, your coat is very shiny today."

Looking sheepish, Ruffshod and Trenton's Pride trotted away behind Sir Trenton. But just before he disappeared over the hillside, Pride turned back to Stripes. "There's a place we can settle this," he said.

"Where and when?" Stripes replied.

"Blue Moon Valley. Tonight," Pride hissed back. "No humans, no rules."

"Son!" Sir Trenton called.

Trenton's Pride turned and galloped away to catch up to his father.

Blue Moon Valley lay hidden amid the quiet Kentucky hills, bordering both the Walsh farm and the Dalrymple estate. A slim spring moon cast long, dark shadows from the trees ringing the valley's central field. A low fog hung above the tall grass, giving the place a mysterious and forbidding feel.

Nearly invisible in the mist were dozens of horses, talking in small groups, waiting for the races to begin. Ruffshod stood next to Trenton's Pride on the side of the clearing closest to the Dalrymple estate. They looked around in every direction.

"See," Ruffshod said. "I told you Stripey wouldn't come."

A huge Clydesdale stepped to the center of the crowd and cleared his throat. All the other horses fell silent.

"Welcome to the Blue Moon Races!" he neighed.

All the other horses cheered and stomped their hooves.

"What's the first and only rule of the Blue Moon Races?" the Clydesdale asked the crowd.

"There are *no* Blue Moon Races!" the audience chorused back.

"Tonight's first contestant is undefeated in ten races," the Clydesdale said. "He's the baddest pony on the prairie. He's lean, he's mean, he's got champ-eeeonn genes. Give it up for . . . Trenton's Pride!"

Pride cantered to the center of the crowd, neighing and shaking his head. He pranced by Sandy, trying to impress her, but the filly merely looked away. The rest of the crowd stomped their hooves and cheered.

"Who's feeling their oats?" the Clydesdale asked the audience. "If you think you're horse enough, step right up!" He scanned the crowd to see if there were any takers. No horse stepped forward.

"I'll take him on!" called a voice from the back of the crowd.

All heads turned as Stripes emerged from the fog. The horses whispered among themselves.

Many of them had not seen this strange, new "horse" before.

Stripes smiled at Sandy. She smiled back at him.

Trenton's Pride approached the zebra. "I'm surprised you showed up," he said.

"You want to *talk*, or race?" Stripes replied.

"Oh, you're going to wish you'd stayed home," Pride snorted.

Stripes was quick to respond. "You're going to wish I'd stayed home, too — after I kick your butt!"

The two of them lined up on either side of the big Clydesdale, who acted as the race's starter and judge. The Clydesdale studied the zebra and made up an introduction on the spot.

"And now for our challenger! He's black, he's white, and apparently not too bright! He's brave and courageous, but his look is outrageous. Let's hear it for . . . the Striped Stranger!"

A smattering of polite hoof stomping ran through the crowd. None of them really knew what to make of Stripes. Only Sandy whinnied loudly.

The Clydesdale nodded toward an abandoned car at the far side of the clearing, barely visible through the fog. "Okay," he bellowed, "up to that heap, around it, and back here. First one back wins."

He raised his voice once more. "Now . . . let's . . ."

As he spoke, all the horses in the valley began stomping their hooves. The noise built to a deafening rumble. "Get ready to race!"

Stripes glanced around, hoping that somebody besides Sandy might be rooting for him. But he was on his own — at least as far as he knew. Stripes didn't see Tucker, who had followed him out to Blue Moon Valley. The old pony was hiding behind a tree to watch the action.

The Clydesdale lifted a red rag from the ground with his mouth and raised it high in the air. All the horses fell silent in anticipation.

The Clydesdale dropped the rag, giving the signal to start. Trenton's Pride surged forward quickly before Stripes even knew what was happening.

"See ya, loser!" Pride called. "Just try and keep up."

"Just giving you a head start — you're going to need it!" Stripes yelled back.

Stripes took off, running as hard as he could. Pride had a good head start, but the zebra's years of racing the mailman and the sunset paid off. He was fast; faster even than the young thoroughbred.

Trenton's Pride glanced back as he neared the junked auto. Stripes was not far behind, and he was gaining fast. Trenton's Pride kicked into high gear, but

Stripes kept right with him. The crowd of horses gasped as the two animals reached the old car, racing almost neck and neck.

"Come on, Pride — is that all you've got?" called Stripes.

Pride snorted. "I haven't even broken a sweat."

Stripes pushed himself to run even harder. "Good thing your daddy's not here to see this!"

"Slow down, kid!" Tucker whispered to himself. "You're gonna blow the turn!"

Trenton's Pride circled the heap like a champion, barely losing any speed as he went.

Stripes shot forward, too, but Tucker was right; he was going too fast. The zebra tried to turn, but he swung wide. His legs shot out from under him and he fell into a nasty skid. He slid through the grass, into a mud puddle, and ended up crashing into some thick bushes at the clearing's edge.

Tucker sighed and shook his head. "He doesn't know what he's doing," he said to himself, "but the kid's got guts."

The other horses cheered as Trenton's Pride sprinted toward the finish line.

Stripes got out of the puddle and tried to get back into the race. He ignored the leaves and mud clinging to his body and ran — but it was no use. It was all over, and he was exhausted.

By the time Trenton's Pride crossed the finish line, Stripes was yards and yards behind him.

The other horses cheered the winner, and laughed when they saw the muddy zebra. Dejected, Stripes didn't even bother to finish. Instead, he turned and headed for home.

"Stripes, are you okay?" Sandy called. But Stripes only mumbled, "Yeah, I'm fine," before hanging his head and walking away. Sandy started after the zebra, but Ruffshod got in her way.

As Trenton's Pride took his victory lap around the other horses, he yelled out after Stripes: "Hey, Stripey! Did you really think you could beat a trained professional?"

As he headed for home, Stripes gazed down at the racetrack below. Now it seemed further away than ever.

CHAPTER

The "Hit" Pelican

Reggie the rooster greeted the next morning the same way he greeted every morning. To the humans, it sounded like "cockle-doodle-do," but the animals understood what he was really saying: "All right, everyone up! No more counting sheep — unless you actually *are* sheep. Get up!"

Channing dragged herself out of the house. She was headed for her part-time job at the racetrack. But she immediately spotted the very filthy zebra.

"Now what did *you* get into last night?" she asked Stripes — though the answer was obviously "mud." She went into the barn and brought back some sponges, towels, and brushes.

"Hey, what's up, boy?" Channing asked. She could see how down Stripes was. "Are you sick or something?"

Stripes was still smarting over his loss in the Blue Moon Race. He just stared at the ground. Trenton's Pride's final insult was lingering in his ears.

"I have a feeling," Channing said, scrubbing him clean, "that there's something you're not telling me."

Stripes didn't look up. He would not be consoled.

Channing gave him a hug. "There. Now you're gorgeous again. I've got to go to work. You stay out of the mud."

She headed for her old motorcycle, parked near the front porch. As she hopped on, Nolan came out of the house. "Helmet!" he called to his daughter.

Channing rolled her eyes. "I'm going to be late for work, dad!" she said. But she pulled on her helmet before kick-starting the engine. Then she roared down the dirt driveway and off to work.

Nolan shook his head and headed back into the house.

U

A pelican circling high above the farm watched as Channing pulled away. He muttered to himself while he flew.

"Boy, would ya get a load of this dump?! Even Old

McDonald wouldn't want this farm. But it's perfect for me . . . miles from the Jersey shore, not an ocean in sight — not even a birdbath. No one will look for a classy guy like me here!" The pelican folded his wings and headed for the open driveway near the barn. The bird miscalculated, though, and came in too low. His tail feathers nearly brushed the top of Reggie's comb.

"Ack!" the rooster cried. "The sky is falling! This is not a drill! Falling sky!"

The pelican crashed into a bale of hay next to the barn, causing a pitchfork and two rakes to clatter to the ground.

Stripes, Franny, and Tucker gaped at the scene of the accident.

The ruffled bird pulled himself out of the mess and staggered across the yard, nearly tripping over his webbed feet. He tried to look casual as he regained his senses.

"That's how we land in the big city," he said in a thick New Jersey accent. "If there's no parking space, you make one. Any of you mugs got a problem with that?"

The Walsh farm animals were still too stunned to say anything.

The pelican gazed around the farm. "Get a load of this dump," he said. "Strictly hicks-burg. Middle-anowheres-ville." He brushed himself off with his wide wings.

Tucker frowned at him. "Nice landing. Can we see you take off now?"

Franny smiled at the newcomer with mock sweetness. "Look, I don't mean to be rude, but you seem to be a little more 'surf' than 'turf.' Did you take a wrong turn?"

"All right, because you look a little slow, I'll skip the salad and get right to the risotto," the pelican replied. "Let's just say I'm having a little disagreement with my family. We disagree about whether or not they should whack me!"

The animals just stared blankly at the new arrival.

"Name's Goose," he said.

"A pelican named Goose?" Tucker scoffed. "That's the stupidest thing I ever heard."

The pelican puffed out his chest and went nose to beak with Tucker. "That's the kind of name they give you when you're the baddest bird on the boardwalk," Goose said defiantly. "When they're too afraid to even look you in the eyes. It's a name that strikes fear into anyone on the East Coast."

Tucker looked Goose straight in the eyes. Just then, Nolan's tractor backfired out in the field. Goose yelped and dove for cover, screaming, "Don't shoot! Don't shoot! I didn't do it! It was the horse with the funny hair! And the goat's in on it, too!"

Tucker rolled his eyes. "You're fine, pal. Unless you're being chased by a backfiring tractor."

Goose stood up and brushed himself off. "Okay, look. Here's the whole spaghetti sauce," he said. "I'm a hit bird. And when Sammy the Gull needs a lesson taught, the Goose is the guy he calls. I was working for Johnny Storkanado. I had this little . . . let's call it a mishap. So I needs a soft spot to hide out for a while."

"Hey, buddy — you ever try shutting up?" Tucker grumbled.

"You ever try swimming in cement horseshoes?" Goose shot back. "I've taken out punks bigger than you!"

"Yeah?" Tucker said. "What'd you do, talk them to death?"

"Hey, be careful, pony boy," Goose said.

Tucker's eyes narrowed. "I should have guessed from the size of that beak that you'd be a big mouth."

"Watch it, Stumpy," Goose replied. "I'd cut you off at the knees, but it looks like somebody's beat me to it."

"Knock it off, you two," Franny said. "We've got better things to do than argue." She was watching Stripes, who had slipped away during the argument. She poked Tucker with her nose and nodded toward Stripes. The zebra was galloping toward Lookout Hill.

Tucker sighed and, after one last glare at the feathery new "addition" to the farm, headed after him.

It took Tucker a while to catch up to Stripes. When he finally did, he found the zebra staring over the fence at the horses training on the Dalrymple estate.

"Hey, kiddo, that's the worst turn I've ever seen anybody make. Awful. Terrible. Stinko," Tucker said.

Stripes spun around. He was surprised that Tucker knew where he had been the night before, but he didn't want to admit anything. "I have no idea what you're talking about," Stripes said.

"Don't worry, kid," Tucker assured him. "The Blue Moon Races are the worst-kept secret of all time."

Stripes gave up his act and gazed back forlornly at the Dalrymple horses. "I almost had him," he said. "I could have beaten him, easily."

"Wrong. It takes hard work to be a racer," Tucker replied.

Nolan Walsh hiked up the hill toward them. He was holding a plow harness. It was time for Stripes to go, so Tucker tried to encourage him one last time. "Nothing ever comes easy, kid. Remember that. And speaking of hard work . . ."

"C'mon," Nolan called. "Time to earn your keep. Tractor is down and I need some help."

Stripes plowed the fields all morning, while the Dalrymple horses — all except Sandy — stood on the other side of the fence and jeered at him.

"Hey, plowboy," Ruffshod shouted, "missed a spot."

When Nolan went inside to take a break, Tucker trotted over to Stripes.

"I'm never going to start training, am I?" Stripes lamented.

"I'm not going to blow sunshine up your tail, kid," Tucker said. "You're from the wrong side of the fence. Only chance you got is if . . ." Tucker broke off. He sighed and shook his head.

"If what?" Stripes asked.

"You gotta get someone to ride you," Tucker said. "Show 'em what you can do."

"A human?" Stripes asked.

"No, we're gonna strap Reggie the rooster on your back," Tucker replied sarcastically. "Of course a human! And if you *do* get the chance to race, you gotta be ready. Pulling this plow will only make you stronger. So put your back into it. Your training can start right here and now. Or, you can give up. It's up to you."

Slowly, Stripes' head — and his spirit — rose. He wasn't a quitter, he decided. "I'm not just going to race," he assured Tucker. "I'm going to win the big race. And then when I walk through this valley, all the other horses will say 'There goes Stripes. He's the best of the best.'"

U

When Nolan returned from the house and grabbed hold of the plow, Stripes took off and almost jerked it right out of his hands. For the rest of the day, Nolan had a hard time keeping up with the eager young zebra.

By sunset, when Channing returned from work, both man and animal were exhausted. Nolan wiped the sweat from his brow as he walked up to the house. Channing parked her motorbike in the barn and gave the zebra a hug. "Who's my best boy?" she asked.

"BAH-WRONK!" the zebra replied.

Channing ruffled his mane then headed into the house for dinner.

Stripes eyed the motorcycle enviously. "Too bad her iron horse won't break like the Chief's digger did," he said. "Then she'd have to ride me."

"That could be arranged," interjected a sly voice.

Stripes was startled to find Goose perched near his haunches. "Who are you?" Stripes asked the bird.

"The name's Goose," Goose replied, checking out the zebra's black and white stripes. "Hey, look, I'm always lookin' to do a favor for someone who's been in the joint. When'd ya get out?"

"Out of where?" asked Stripes.

"The pokey. The do-right ranch. The iron-bar inn. Come on, you can level with me," Goose said.

Stripes sighed, confused. "What are you talking about?"

"Oh, you're good!" said Goose. "Very good! So where'd you do your stretch, huh? Sing-Sing? Alcatraz? The Bronx Zoo?"

"Look, how can you help?" Stripes cut in.

Tucker and Franny and Reggie were curious about the meeting between Stripes and Goose — and a little anxious, too. They had all known Stripes since he was tiny, and they were still very protective of him. But it didn't bother Goose that they gathered around him. He worked better in front of a crowd.

"That's right," Goose said. "Any bird ruffled their feathers, they'd just call the Goose and bada bing, bada boom. It was done. Bye-bye birdie."

Reggie bought Goose's entire act. "You're a hit bird?" he guessed.

Goose chose to not answer, to heighten the intrigue.

"He's a looney bird," Tucker said. He and Fanny were skeptical.

"Don't listen to Stumpy over there," Goose assured Stripes. "I've got connections. You scratch my back, I'll scratch yours. All right, listen up! Professor Goose is gonna school ya in 'How to Take Out a Motorcycle.' Class is now in session."

Reggie looked panicked. "Will we be tested on this?" he asked.

"Stuff it, McNugget!" Goose replied. "Rule number one: we never say nothin' — not a word gets out!" He looked around, cautiously. "It's time. You guys stay here. This ain't gonna be pretty."

Stripes still wasn't sure exactly what the bird meant. After nightfall, though, he spotted the pelican sneaking around outside the barn.

Reggie paced around the barn, nervous. "Gentlemen, don't let the feathers fool you. That dude is dangerous! He's a hit man disguised as an idiot!"

A few minutes later, a huge CRASH shook the barnyard. One of the motorbike's wheels sailed past the barn door, followed closely by a very confused-looking pelican.

Goose staggered into the barn, his face and feathers black and scorched. "See?" he said. "You call the Goose and bada bing . . ."

But before he could finish the sentence, the pelican fell flat on his long beak.

Tucker chuckled and finished for him. ". . . bada *boom*."

CHAPTER

On Zebraback

The next morning, Channing and her dad examined the remains of the motorbike.

"Well," Nolan said, "you won't be riding to work on *this* any time soon. What happened? It looks like lightning hit it."

"I have no idea, but I'm going to be *late*," Channing said.

Nolan reached into his pocket and handed his daughter the keys to the truck. Stripes and the other animals watched from nearby.

The farmer and the teenager stopped dead next to the blue pickup. The right front tire looked like a pancake — flat, all the way to the ground.

Goose, perched nearby, winked at the other animals. He had thought of everything.

"That's just great," Channing sighed. "How long will it take to put on the spare?"

Nolan scratched his head. "That *is* the spare. It'll take me a while to patch it up."

Frustrated, Channing cast her eyes up to the sky. When she looked back down, she found Stripes staring hopefully at her. The zebra nudged her with his nose.

"Hey, Dad . . ." Channing said. "Could I take Stripes? Just for today?"

Nolan laughed. "*Ride* Stripes?" he said. "Not on your life."

"But I have to get to work," she pleaded. "Come on, Dad. Can I take him, please?"

"It's not like he's just any old horse, Channing," Nolan said. "I'll never be able to get a saddle on him."

"Dad, please?" Channing said. "Just try. He pulled the plow."

Nolan looked skeptical, but — inside of five minutes — he had the zebra saddled and ready to go.

The farmer scratched his head again. "Well, okay. So I got a saddle on him. But he'll never let you ride."

Channing smiled at her dad. "You don't know him like I do," she replied.

"Look, Channing," Nolan said, "even if he *does* let

you — you know how I feel about you riding. Your mom . . ."

"Dad, I was riding when I was five," Channing reminded him.

"That's not the point."

"Come on," she said encouragingly. "It's almost like he *wants* to be ridden. Just let me try."

Nolan rubbed his chin, feeling unsure. Before he could make up his mind, Channing hopped onto Stripes' back. The zebra looked wobbly at first, and he nearly stumbled.

The farmer rushed forward. "Careful!" he cried.

"I'm okay, dad. He's just getting used to it," Channing said.

"I don't like this at all, Channing."

"I won't go too fast," Channing replied. "I promise."

Nolan sighed. "Nothing more than a *trot* the whole way. Do you understand?"

"But I'll be late," she protested.

"Yes you will," he said. "And don't forget your helmet."

As the teenager ran to get her helmet, Tucker and Franny pulled the zebra aside.

"Not too fast," Franny cautioned. "Take your time."

Tucker just smiled. "Will you be quiet? I'm the coach — you're the goat. Now listen to the ways it's done. Run like the wind, kid. Show her what you got." He turned to Franny. "*That's* coaching."

Channing waved good-bye to her father as she and Stripes slowly made their way toward the track. The zebra's trot became more confident with each and every step.

As soon as they'd passed out of sight of the house, Channing couldn't help herself. She jiggled the reins, encouraging Stripes to go faster. "Come on, boy!" she said, "giddyup."

Stripes took off like a bolt of lightning, galloping down the road toward the racetrack. Soon, Channing and Stripes moved together like one cohesive unit, totally in sync. In no time at all, they arrived at Turfway Park — the Home of Champions. The two of them ignored the surprised looks both human and animal strangers shot their way.

"I'll see you at the end of the day, buddy," Channing said. She tied Stripes to one of the stalls.

But the other horses in the stable jeered the zebra. "Go back to where you belong," they said. "No freaks allowed!"

Stripes knew he couldn't stand there all day listening to them. So he used his teeth to unlatch the reins and hurried off to find Charming.

But the racing compound proved larger than he expected, and he quickly lost sight of her. The zebra made his way to the side of the track and stood next to Woodzie, a rumpled man sitting half-asleep in a chair. Everyone around the track knew Woodzie. He practically lived there. And so did the two horseflies perched on the brim of Woodzie's tattered hat. When they saw Stripes, both horseflies did a double-take.

"Hey, Buzz," one of the flies said to the other, "I've got ten thousand eyes and none of them are working. That looks like a striped horse."

"Make that twenty thousand, Scuzz," the other half of the horsefly duo responded. "I'm seeing it too. Must be the racetrack referee. Let's get a closer look."

Buzz and Scuzz took off from Woodzie's hat. They couldn't really stand each other, but without one another, they'd both be lost. They landed on the rail in front of Stripes.

"Hey, why the long face?" Scuzz said to break the ice. Stripes just ignored him.

"Don't you get it? You're a horse. You all have long faces." The flies laughed hysterically.

"I've heard all the jokes," Stripes replied without breaking a smile. "All I know is that I'm different."

"You think you've had it rough?" Buzz shot back. "Try starting out life as a maggot. Nobody wants to pet a little maggot. Nobody!"

"Here we go again with the sob stories," Scuzz said. "He blames all his problems on his childhood."

Stripes couldn't help but like these two. "I'm Stripes," he offered.

"That's the greatest news I ever heard," Buzz said with a sigh of relief. "We thought we were going blind, or maybe crazy."

"Yeah," Scuzz agreed. "I saw ya, and I was about to say to my buddy Buzz here, I've never seen a black horse with white stripes before, ya know?"

"You dimwit!" Buzz exploded. "He is obviously a white horse with black stripes. Anybody can see that."

Nearby, Channing swept up garbage. She was so busy at her job, she didn't notice the zebra. Not until Clara Dalrymple tapped her on the shoulder.

"Who does that . . . *thing* belong to?" Clara asked, pointing to Stripes.

Channing smiled sheepishly. "He's mine, Ms. Dalrymple. My transportation broke down. I didn't have any other way to —"

"From now on," the millionairess interrupted, "leave *it* up at that petting zoo that you and your father laughably call a farm. This is a racetrack, not Africa."

She turned away from the zebra and carefully examined the area Channing had just been cleaning. Ms. Dalrymple brushed one white-gloved hand across the railing and frowned. "This rail looks rather dingy," she said. "You know how I like things to sparkle. Have the whole rail — all the way around the track — wiped down before you leave tonight."

Channing swallowed her anger. "Yes, Ms. Dalrymple."

Clara Dalrymple marched off. Channing tied Stripes to the railing.

"Just hang out here, okay?" she said to the zebra. "Don't get me into any more trouble." As she went back to work, Trenton's Pride and Ruffshod sauntered up to the rail.

"Well, well, well . . ." Ruffshod said. "If it ain't Mr. Four-Left-Hooves."

Stripes held his head high. "I'm here to train." He nodded toward Channing. "That's my rider."

Trenton's Pride whinnied a harsh laugh. "The trash cleaner?" he said. "She's barely fit to *clean* the track, never mind ride on it."

Stripes' eyes narrowed with anger. "Don't talk about my girl like that!"

Trenton's Pride laughed again. "Try to remember which side of that rail you belong on, freak," he told Stripes.

He and Ruffshod kept on laughing as their exercise riders led them away.

Stripes tried to stay positive, but Pride's words haunted him. "Maybe I am just fooling myself," he thought. "Maybe this is as close to the track as I'm ever going to get. After all, I'm too small and I certainly don't look like any of the other horses."

Just then, Trenton's Pride and Ruffshod rushed by at full speed. The wind from their passing blew in Stripes' face. Just the feel of the wind in his face made Stripes determined to run again.

"There's your Open winner, Ms. D," John Cooper told Mrs. Dalrymple. He was the trainer who had replaced Nolan a few years ago.

"He'd better be, " she replied. "Anything less than a victory and you'll be back to shoveling manure."

Woodzie stopped "sleeping" just long enough to

check the time on his stopwatch as Pride roared past. He nodded, then pulled his hat down over his eyes once more.

Channing watched for a moment, too. Stripes sensed that Channing felt the same as he did and wished he could do more for her . . . and maybe he could.

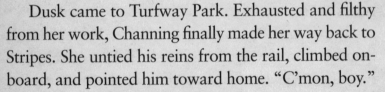

Dusk came to Turfway Park. Exhausted and filthy from her work, Channing finally made her way back to Stripes. She untied his reins from the rail, climbed on-board, and pointed him toward home. "C'mon, boy."

Stripes strode in the opposite direction — toward the track.

No matter how hard Channing pulled, Stripes would not be deterred. He took Channing through a break in the fence and onto the main oval.

Channing glanced around, worried. "What are you doing?" Channing hissed. "We can't be out here!"

Stripes rode toward the middle of the track. He bowed his neck and pranced, feeling lighter than air. Channing took a deep breath.

"I know how you feel, boy," she said. "When I was little, my mom used to bring me out here. She'd put me on the saddle behind her and take me once around the track — the whole thing. It was like magic."

Instinctively, she leaned forward, into a jockey's riding position. She shook the reins at Stripes.

Zoom! Stripes shot forward. The two of them rocketed down the straightaway. Except for her piston-like arms, not a muscle on the young girl's body moved. She rode like she'd been doing it all her life.

Channing pulled up Stripes at the end of the straightaway and decided not to press their luck. She spotted the exit and steered Stripes toward it.

As they reached the break in the rail, Woodzie stepped into their path.

"Channing," he said. "Hold on a sec."

"Woodzie!" she replied. "You scared me! You're not going to tell anyone, are you?"

The rumpled track veteran put one finger to his lips. "Mum's the word," he said. "Who's your friend? He's pretty quick."

"This is Stripes," Channing said. "Do you really think he's fast?"

Woodzie nodded as Buzz and Scuzz watched the action from the brim of his hat. "Yeah, I do. Maybe really fast," the wily, old track veteran said. "I'd like to time him for real."

"Are you kidding? My dad would kill me," Channing replied. "He doesn't want me to *ride*, let along race. And we can't race a zebra, anyway."

Woodzie shook his head. "That's a crime," he said. "You move just like your mom — God rest her soul. Tell you what, a trainer friend of mine's got a couple of horses working tomorrow. Show up early and join in."

"Ms. Dalrymple told me to keep Stripes at home," Channing said.

"Ah, the dragon lady's too busy to notice," Woodzie replied. "Let's see how he does first. You can tell your dad afterwards — if there's anything to tell."

Slowly, Channing Walsh nodded and smiled. The thought of entering a race — even a practice race — made her spirit soar.

CHAPTER

Lunch for a Lion

Nolan Walsh sat at the kitchen table, waiting by the phone. It was late and Channing should have been home ages ago. He almost didn't hear his daughter as she sneaked in the front door and headed upstairs. Almost.

"Hey," he called to her. "Forget where we live?"

Channing let out a silent sigh and headed for the kitchen. "Ms. Dalrymple made me stay late," she said. "I can't stand her."

"That's no excuse for not calling," Nolan said.

"She gave me extra duties because I took Stripes to the track. She doesn't like him. But why should she," Channing added, "she doesn't even like horses. You can tell."

Nolan shook his head and sighed. "When Clara

looks at a horse, she doesn't see the beauty like we do. It's all business to her — all about money in her pocket."

Channing nodded. "I don't know how you stood it, working for her all those years."

"Sure, she was a pain," Nolan replied, "but I got to work with some mighty fine horses."

Channing saw the glimmer return in her dad's eyes. "Dad," Channing said, "we could do it again. We could train a winner and maybe even take the Kentucky Open."

"That's all in the past, honey. I'm a farmer, now," Nolan said with false enthusiasm. He quickly changed the subject. "Hey, I fixed the flat. You can take the truck tomorrow."

"But I want to ride Stripes again," Channing said. "He was great. You should have seen him."

Nolan arched his eyebrows at his daughter. "Oh?"

Channing looked away, knowing her dad had figured out she and Stripes had done more than just trot.

"Riding Stripes to work was a one-shot deal," Nolan said. "You know how I feel."

"But, Dad . . ." Channing began.

Nolan cut her off. "I said *no*, Channing."

She bit her lip, so as not to burst into tears, and

then it all rushed out of her. "You're so busy trying to keep me from hurting myself like Mom did that you never give me a chance to try anything. Well, just because you've given up on your dreams doesn't mean I have to!"

Channing turned and stormed outside, slamming the door behind her. She found Stripes in the barn and hugged him.

"Dad treats me like I'm still a little girl. Well, I'm not. He always tells me that I'm so special, and then he wants me to be like everybody else."

Stripes nodded his head and snorted, almost as if he understood. Then he nuzzled up against Channing's cheek.

"Why can't he understand me like you do?" Channing asked Stripes. She looked determined. "I don't care what he says," she proclaimed. "I want to race and I'm *going* to race. And no one can stop me."

She gazed up to where her mom's riding saddle — unused since her death when Channing was a little girl — hung on the barn wall. Stripes looked at it, too.

"Tomorrow," Channing said softly, "we're going to use that for more than just a wall ornament."

Channing woke before sunrise and sneaked out of the house. As she put her mom's saddle on Stripes, she held a finger to her lips. "Shhh," she cautioned Stripes as they rode away. "Don't make a sound."

When they arrived at Turfway Park, many Kentucky Open hopefuls sauntered around the track, working out. It was media day. Reporters and race fans swarmed the grounds, thrilled to get a glimpse of the finest racehorses in the world.

Meanwhile, the two horseflies, Buzz and Scuzz were goofing off, as usual. Scuzz had fallen into Woodzie's coffee cup and was doing the backstroke.

"Get out of there, Scuzz!" Buzz hissed. "That's the man's espresso!"

Scuzz grinned. "I know I'm 'espressin'' myself!"

"*You* are the reason they invented flyswatters," Buzz grumbled.

On the track, dozens of photographers surrounded Sir Trenton, who posed for pictures next to Clara Dalrymple, Kentucky's first lady of horseracing. The last thing anyone expected to see was a zebra lining up in the backstretch. The reporters and photographers turned their attention from Clara Dalrymple and Trenton's Pride and ran to position themselves for a shot of Stripes.

Clara Dalrymple fumed. "That little Walsh brat's as stubborn as her father. They're turning this place into a three-ring circus." She stormed away, heading for the stands.

Woodzie spotted Ms. Dalrymple, but decided not to mention her to Channing. He rubbed Stripes' nose. "All warmed up?" he asked the zebra and his rider. "Ready to do it?"

Channing nodded nervously. "I guess."

Woodzie winked and headed back toward Clocker's Corner — the part of the racetrack used for timing horses. "Knock 'em dead, kid!"

Buzz and Scuzz circled Woodzie's hat, then flew over the track to get a better view.

Stripes felt nervous waiting in the starter's gate. The other horses in the gate glared at the zebra, not sure what to make of him.

"It's okay, Stripes," Channing said, patting his side.

The bell clanged and the gate flew open. Stripes got off a step slow.

Channing pulled on the reins and urged the zebra forward. Stripes dug in and ran hard.

He started far behind the pack, but gained on them quickly. The other four riders glanced back as the zebra shifted into high gear.

As they passed Clocker's Corner, Channing saw a blue pickup pulling into the parking lot — her dad's truck. Her father had figured out what she was up to. Channing Walsh gritted her teeth, knowing the punishment to come would be stiff.

"C'mon, boy!" she whispered. "We can't get into any more trouble than we already have. Let's show 'em what you can do." She took aim at the pack, trying to find a spot to squeeze through.

Sweat beaded on Stripes' forehead. Dirt and thundering hooves flew all around him. Stripes had never been this close to this many horses. He felt trapped. At any moment, he might be kicked or crushed.

He pulled back — too quickly. His front legs reared up and he came to an abrupt stop.

"Whoa!" Channing gasped. She lost her grip on the reins and tumbled hard onto the track.

"Channing! Chan!" Nolan shouted. He ducked under the outer rail and sprinted toward his daughter.

Channing got up gingerly and dusted herself off. "I'm all right, Dad," she said. "No big deal. Nothing's broken."

Her father looked both scared and angry. Clara approached Nolan and Channing. "The track is no place for a little girl," Clara Dalrymple said. She looked happy as she said it.

"He just got spooked," Channing said to her father. "It's not his fault. He just needs more training."

"He does, or his rider does?" Clara said scornfully. "Like mother, like daughter, eh?"

Nolan Walsh went red in the face. "Get Stripes and meet me in the parking lot," he told Channing.

Channing started to say something, but stopped. She grabbed Stripes' reins and headed for the parking lot. Nolan turned to Clara Dalrymple.

"Clara," he said. "Don't you ever bring up my wife again, and don't you ever speak to my daughter that way again."

By now, reporters were closing in on them. Clara put on a gracious smile. "Really, Nolan," she said, "do you expect me to dignify that with a reply? I'm just a Kentucky gal who loves watching thoroughbreds racing at the top of their form. You can quote me on that," she said to the reporters.

"You don't know the difference between a horse and a donkey," Nolan said.

"At least I know the difference between a horse and a zebra," Clara replied. She arched one carefully-painted eyebrow. "My, how low you've sunk since I fired you."

Nolan decided to not take the bait. Woodzie, on the other hand, loved to stir things up. He had just arrived, and he couldn't wait to get in on the action. Clara's head trainer, John Cooper, was next to him.

"You didn't fire him, he quit," Woodzie roared from the back of the crowd.

No one spoke that way to Clara Dalrymple. All the cameras turned to find the culprit. Woodzie stood his ground.

"And you are?" a reporter asked.

"Robert C. Woods. Folks call me Woodzie."

"He's just a track rat," John Cooper interjected.

Woodzie was undaunted. "Hey, Clara," he said, "what's your quote about why you ain't won the open since Nolan *quit* training for you?"

Clara smiled, but her lips were white. "I'll tell you what . . ." Clara said, playing to the reporters. "As head of the Turfway Board, I am extending an invitation for Mr. Walsh to enter a horse in the Kentucky Open any time he wants . . . for half price. Maybe he'd like to enter his zebra?"

Nolan ignored her challenge and turned and headed for the parking lot.

"There goes the great Nolan Walsh," Clara said as soon as the cameras were turned off, "corn farmer and zebra trainer."

Woodzie remembered something and pulled his

Baby zebra Stripes is accidentally abandoned by his traveling circus troupe.

A young girl
named Channing
and her father,
Nolan, come to
Stripes' rescue.

The other animals at Nolan's farm help take care of the baby zebra, too.

Stripes finds a friend in Sandy, a beautiful pony from the ranch next door.

But not all the horses at the neighboring farm are as friendly as Sandy. A Clydesdale is jealous of Stripes.

Stripes wants to race, too. So he accepts the horse's challenge to race in secret, at night.

Stripes loses his first race — but he's not about to let that stop him. So he finds a rider in Channing.

Stripes and Channing are determined to win the Kentucky Open — no matter what the odds. Or where they have to train!

Finally, it's time for the big race.
And Stripes wins by a nose!

It's a photo finish for Channing and Stripes!

stopwatch from his pocket. When he looked at the watch, a wry smile lit up his face.

Channing sat, head in hands, on the bumper of the old truck, waiting for her father. Stripes stood by the rail of the warm-up paddock. Sir Trenton sauntered up to him.

"See what happens," the big horse said, "when one forgets one's station? The racetrack is no place for a zebra."

Stripes' emotions changed from sadness to puzzlement. "What did you just call me?" he asked.

"A *zebra*," Sir Trenton replied. "Are you as stupid as you are ugly? You didn't really think you were a *horse*, did you?"

"But . . . I *am* a horse," Stripes said desperately. "A *race*horse. I just look a little different."

A superior smile crept across Sir Trenton's muzzle. "You are nothing of the kind," he said. "You are lunch for a lion and not much use for anything else. And you will *never* be a racehorse." He turned, swished his tail in Stripes' face, and walked away.

CHAPTER

Memories and Dreams

Channing and Nolan Walsh hardly glanced at each other as Nolan drove the pickup back toward their farm. They went slowly so Stripes, tethered to the back gate, could walk beside the truck.

"I can't believe you deliberately disobeyed me!" Nolan fumed.

"Mom would have let me ride," Channing said. "I know she would."

"Don't bring your mother into this conversation," Nolan said.

"Why not?" Channing shot back. "At least she would have *tried* to understand. That's more than I can say for you." She suddenly opened the passenger-side door and hopped out.

Nolan hit the brakes. Channing unhooked Stripes

from the back of the truck, hopped aboard her mother's saddle, and rode away.

Her father called after her to stop, but Channing didn't listen. She and the zebra cut over the fields toward the Walsh farm.

Nolan shook his head and drove home. When he got there, he was relieved to find Stripes grazing in the yard. Nolan caught a glimpse of Channing in her bedroom window, but she darted away when she spotted him.

The farmer sighed and went about the business of working the farm.

Toward evening, Woodzie's battered jalopy pulled up the drive. The track veteran stopped in front of the house and got out. He tipped his hat to Nolan, and the two horseflies — Buzz and Scuzz — took off from the brim.

"Hey, we made it, man!" cried Scuzz.

"*We* made it," Buzz replied, looking at the windshield of Woodzie's truck, "but little Skeeter here didn't."

Scuzz checked out the squished mosquito on the windshield. "Oh, no!" he said. "That's why Mom always said to look both ways before crossing!"

"Hey, Woodzie," Nolan said as Woodzie approached. "What brings you out here?"

"I got this wild idea," Woodzie said. "You see, there's nothing in the rules for the Open that says a thoroughbred's the only thing that can run. I checked. Any animal belonging to the genus equus can enter."

Nolan wiped the sweat from his brow. "So what?"

"Clara personally invited you to enter," Woodzie continued. "You can't refuse a challenge like that."

"She only made the offer to humiliate me," Nolan said. "That zebra may be quick over a short distance, but a mile and a quarter . . . ? Come on."

Woodzie pulled a battered stopwatch out of his pocket and showed it to Nolan. "I know he didn't finish, but I got him at half a mile," Woodzie said.

The farmer scratched his head. "Forty two flat for a half mile?" he said. "That's hard to believe. That's flying."

"I ain't touched it since this morning," Woodzie said. "*Forty two flat;* your zebra. By the way, working him was my idea — not Channing's."

"That's beside the point," Nolan said. "She needs to accept responsibility for her actions."

"That zebra wants to race," Woodzie said. "I can see it. *You* just need to train him. You're still the best I've ever seen, Nolan," Woodzie said.

Stripes and Tucker, grazing nearby, looked expectantly at Nolan.

"Where would we train him?" Nolan replied. "And even if we could, I don't have the five-thousand-dollar entrance fee."

"I do," Woodzie said. "I won a lot of it betting on your horses. Your wife rode most of 'em. I feel like I kind of owe it to you."

Nolan started to shake his head, but Woodzie cut him off. "I know a good bet when I see one. But I can't bet on the zebra if he's not in the race. And Channing . . . well, I've never seen anyone her age sit that chilly in the saddle. Rides just like her mom."

"That's just what I'm afraid of," Nolan said. He turned and walked back into the house.

Woodzie sighed. He strolled back to his jalopy and drove away.

Buzz and Scuzz had been listening the whole time, and now Scuzz began to rant. "Whoa! He's not gonna let Stripes race — that's not cool!" The flies took off for the barn.

When they arrived, they landed on Tucker's nose.

"Hey! How you been, fellas?" Tucker asked.

Scuzz grinned. "We sure miss ya down at the track, Tucker."

"Ahh, those were some great years," Tucker sighed.

Buzz interrupted. "Yeah, yeah. Listen, we've got some bad news for Stripes."

Goose waddled over to the flies. "Let me guess: his parole officer's caught up with him?" He turned to Stripes. "Don't let them take you alive, kid!"

"Is he always like this?" Buzz asked Tucker.

Tucker rolled his eyes. "Worse. Much worse."

Buzz looked back at Stripes. "Anyway, listen, kid," he said. "The Chief isn't gonna let you race."

"But don't worry about that," Scuzz added. "We'll cheer you up!" The two flies burst into song, dancing on Stripes' back. But Stripes just shook them off and walked away.

"Stripes!" Franny called. "Walking away isn't going to solve anything!"

But Stripes didn't turn around. "Who cares?" he answered.

"We've gotta get this kid into the race!" Buzz said, turning to Tucker.

Tucker sighed. "Not a chance. The Chief will never go for it."

"Of course he will," Franny said. "Just like somebody else I know. He just needs a little push."

Later, after the stars came out, Nolan Walsh sat on the porch. In his hand he held a stack of unpaid bills. Nolan didn't have a clue how to make the farm prosperous, but something else bothered him even more. He didn't have a clue how to be a good father to a teenage girl. He missed his wife every day, but tonight he missed her even more than usual. *She would know what to do with Channing,* he thought.

Nolan contemplated a just punishment. He knew something had to be done.

Nolan and Channing hadn't spoken since she jumped out of the truck. But as she headed from the barn back into the house, she mumbled. "Good night, Dad. I'm going to bed."

Nolan stood and put his hand on the screen door, keeping her from opening it.

"Big day today," he said.

"Yeah."

"Big problem, too. What do you think we ought to do about it?"

She looked at him sadly. "I don't know."

Nolan sighed. "I think the only thing to do is to re-move the problem."

"No!" Channing said, tears welling up in her eyes. "It's not his fault, dad. Stripes is not the problem. He doesn't know any better. It's *my* fault. Please, Dad, don't send him to the zoo. I love him."

Nolan crossed his arms over his chest. "Well, what's the alternative, then?"

Channing's lower lip quivered. "That I don't ride him again," she said softly.

"That's right," Nolan replied.

"Not ever?" she asked, devastated at the thought.

"Not ever. You stepped over the line today. Way over."

"I know," Channing sobbed. Her dad let go of the door and she ran up to her room, crying.

Nolan went back to his bills — but he still couldn't see any way out.

A half hour later, a clatter from the barn caught his attention.

"Now what the . . ." he began. Then he slapped his forehead. "Of course, the pelican. We'll probably get some baboons next. Then maybe a nice dolphin in the creek. . . ."

He laid aside his paperwork and headed for the barn door. As he got there, Franny pushed it open for him. Nolan looked questioningly at the goat.

"Maaaa!" Franny bleated.

"If only you could talk," Nolan said wistfully.

As the farmer went inside, Tucker came up and

nudged him toward the tack room, where the riding gear was stored. Stripes, Franny, Reggie, and most of the other farm animals followed behind them.

Nolan gave the old Shetland pony a puzzled look. "What's up, Tucker?" he said. "What's going on, boy?"

Tucker went to the side of the room and pulled away a piece of cloth. At the same time, Reggie flicked on the light.

On the wall of the barn hung a series of pictures and mementos from the glory days of the Walsh farm. Nolan hadn't looked in this room for a very long time.

A picture of Channing riding a horse as a toddler hung on the left. Next to it was a picture of her mother sitting astride the Kentucky Open winner. Five-year-old Channing sat smiling on her lap. Nolan, grinning from ear-to-ear, held the horse's reins.

Tucker looked back and forth from Nolan to the pictures. Nolan followed the pony's gaze and understood. Tears welled up in the farmer's eyes.

He knelt down and hugged the pony. "Thanks, buddy," he whispered.

Channing whimpered as she lay in bed. Her eyes were red and swollen from crying so hard. Then she heard something outside and went to the window to investigate.

When she looked outside, she didn't believe her eyes. Under a full moon, her father was plowing under the corn crop they'd worked so hard to plant. Her dad grinned from ear to ear as he mowed the leafy green stalks down in a regular oval pattern — a racetrack.

Channing Walsh zoomed down the stairs, ran out of the house, jumped up on the tractor and gave her father a big hug.

Stripes, Tucker, Franny, Reggie, and Goose watched the humans. All of them smiled.

"If you build it, they will come," said Reggie.

Tucker looked at the racetrack, then at Stripes. "Welcome to the big time, kid. You ready to start training?"

But Stripes just hung his head. "Why bother?" he asked as he fled into the barn.

CHAPTER

Paying the Price

Later, Nolan Walsh pulled on Stripes' reins as Channing sat astride the zebra's back. The two of them tried to coax Stripes into a makeshift starting gate they'd set up near the course.

"We'll have to work on stamina more than speed," Nolan said. "Zebras burn up adrenaline much faster than horses. That's because they have a heightened flight reflex from being hunted on the plains of Africa."

Channing just grinned at him.

"What?" he said. "You're not the only one who knows how to use the Internet. Before we work on that, though, we need to get him used to this gate."

"Easy boy," Channing said to the zebra. "Easy does it."

Stripes began circling and kicking, doing whatever he could to stay out of the gate.

"Channing, back off," Nolan said. "Let's give him a minute to calm down. Then we'll try again."

Channing got off the zebra's back and Stripes trotted away into the cornfield.

Tucker and Franny, watching from nearby, went after him. "I thought you wanted this," the pony called after the zebra.

Stripes turned. "I do, but . . . I don't belong in the gate."

"Don't give me excuses," Tucker said. "Racing is for contenders. Champions. It's for any horse with a fire in his heart. Maybe you don't have what it takes? Maybe you just talk a good game?"

Stripes scowled at the Shetland pony. "What do you know, anyway, you little nobody? You never raced!" He trotted back to the track, where Nolan intercepted him.

"Come on," the farmer said. "Back to work."

After an unsuccessful workout, Stripes wandered up by the creek, grazing and looking morose.

"Excuse me," said a friendly voice, "have you seen

a guy called Stripes? He looks a lot like you, but happier."

Stripes looked up. "Oh, great. More jokes. I really just want to be alone, Sandy."

"What's going on with you?" the filly asked. "This is what you've always wanted, but you're sure not acting like a champion."

"That's because I'm *not* a racehorse," Stripes replied bitterly. "I'm not even a regular horse. I'm a . . ."

"Zebra," Sandy put in. "I know. I've traveled the world. Remember?"

"Why didn't you say anything?" Stripes asked.

"Because it doesn't matter to me. You love to run, and that's all that matters," Sandy replied.

"To you, maybe," Stripes said. "Because it's not *your* problem."

"If you want to see the *real* problem," Sandy said, "try looking down." She galloped off.

Stripes did. His reflection gazed back up at him from the stream. Angry, Stripes galloped away.

Back at the barn, Stripes kicked at the straw on the floor as he headed for his stall.

". . . Maybe you don't have what it takes!" he said to himself, mocking Tucker. "Maybe you just talk a good game. Who does he think he is, anyway? What's *he* ever done? He didn't even know that I'm a zebra!"

Franny stepped out of the shadows. The old nanny goat looked angry. "That's enough out of you, young colt," she said. She nodded toward the pictures hanging on the tack room wall. "Take a look up there. What do you see?"

Stripes refused to look. "I've seen 'em before. The Chief, my girl and her mother, different horses."

"What else?" Franny said. "Look a little lower, behind everyone."

Stripes went closer to the pictures and looked. In the background of every picture, outside of the winner's circle, stood Tucker.

"He trained them all," Franny said. "Trained every champion, right alongside the Chief. Not one of them ever, *ever* thanked him. But Tucker believes in you. Now you have to believe in him."

Stripes suddenly felt like a fool. "Do you know where he is?" he asked Franny.

"Lookout Hill, last I saw," the goat replied.

The zebra ran up to Lookout Hill as fast as his legs would carry him. He found the old Shetland pony standing alone atop the rise.

"Franny told me about you training the big race champions," Stripes said, gasping for air. "Why didn't you say anything?"

"Talk's cheap," Tucker replied.

"I'm sorry for the way I've been acting," Stripes said. "I'm the last one who should be name calling. It's just . . . I found out I'm not really a racehorse. I'm a zebra."

"So what?" Tucker replied. "To me, you're just a horse with stripes who needs an attitude adjustment."

"Tucker," Stripes said tentatively, "you don't really think I have what it takes . . . to be a champion?"

Tucker looked sternly at him. "I'm the only horse I've ever seen that's got shorter legs than you. And you don't have the size or strength or natural ability of Trenton's Pride or Ruffshod . . ."

Stripes hung his head.

"But you've got more heart than both of them put together," Tucker finished. "I wouldn't trade you for either one of them."

Stripes' head popped back up. *Franny was right*, he thought. *Tucker really does believe in me.*

The next day, they went back to work.

"That's what I'm talking about!" Tucker called as Stripes and Channing rounded the corner. They were so close to the edge of the "track" that the teenager's sleeves almost brushed the corn stalks.

Nolan slapped Woodzie on the back. "Will you look at that!" he said. "We might actually have a chance."

Woodzie looked starry-eyed. "If we're lucky, maybe at a hundred-to-one."

"Now if he can just learn to come out of the gate," Nolan said.

"That's no problem," Woodzie said. "You've worked with every kind of horse there is."

Nolan sighed. "The problem is, he's not a horse."

"If anyone can do it, Nolan, you can," Woodzie said. "I'm counting on it."

They practiced hard all day. And the day after that. And the day after that, too.

The weeks became a blur of training and hard running. Getting Stripes used to the gate was tough, but Nolan used every trick he knew. The farmer-turned-trainer even tied his shirt onto a rake to imitate the sound of the racetrack pennants flapping in the breeze.

Every day Stripes worked, Tucker knew that Trenton's Pride was working just as hard in the ultra-modern Dalrymple stables. Where Stripes had a cornfield, Pride had a real racetrack. Where Stripes had a gate made of old farm parts and rope, Pride's facility had state-of-the-art, computer-controlled gates. Where Stripes had Lookout Hill, Pride had a treadmill.

But Stripes had one thing that Trenton's Pride didn't — Channing. Her mother had been a champion jockey. Now, as race day approached, the teenager tried on a new riding outfit — silks she'd made especially to look like the ones her mother Carolyn had worn.

Tucker gazed down the hill at Turfway Park. From years of experience, he knew what the special preparations at the track meant.

"Tomorrow's the big day, kid," Tucker said to Stripes.

"Do you think I'm ready?" the zebra asked.

"Absolutely," Tucker said. "Remember, when you turn the corner and you're headed for the finish line, your legs will be burning up; on fire. That's when you have to reach down inside yourself and find out what you're made of. Like I used to tell all my other racers — *don't look back, leave it all on the track*."

"What's that mean?" Stripes said.

Tucker chuckled. "When the time is right," he said, "you'll know."

That night, while Stripes worked, all the other animals — Tucker, Franny, Goose, Reggie, and even the flies, Buzz and Scuzz — talked about ways to help their friend during the race. They discussed things they might do to give Stripes the edge over Trenton's Pride, Ruffshod, and the others the zebra would be racing against.

After all the rest had bedded down, Stripes tiptoed toward the barn door.

Franny opened one eye. "Going somewhere?" she asked.

"I need to make things right with Sandy," Stripes replied.

The old goat smiled understandingly.

Stripes headed for the creek. It was a beautiful night. And Sandy was there, gazing at the stars.

"Why the long face?" Stripes asked.

Sandy looked at him, not amused.

"You're a horse," Stripes explained. "Long face . . . get it?"

"I've heard it," Sandy replied. "It's lame." She looked longingly at him. "I was hoping you'd come."

"I'm sorry that . . ." they both said.

"You first," Sandy said.

"I was wrong for what I said," Stripes said.

"No argument there," Sandy replied. "I just got mad at you because . . . well, because I care so much. You're so *lucky* to be where you are."

"This old place?" Stripes said. "The Chief is barely

holding it together. You have the best farm in the world. The best of everything."

"Yeah," Sandy said, "but I don't have any friends. Not real friends, like you have. A friend like I bet you are."

"Listen, Sandy, I know I don't look like a race-horse, but —" Stripes started to say.

Sandy laughed. "Oh, stop! I care more about what's on the inside, and you have more on the inside than *any* of the horses over here. Plus, I happen to think that what you have on the outside is the cutest thing on four hooves. Just so you know, I'm already on your side."

"Oh, isn't that just precious," neighed a deep, booming voice. "Beauty and the Beast."

Sandy and Stripes jumped as Sir Trenton, Ruff-shod, and a dozen other horses surrounded them from all sides. "Oh, no," whispered Sandy. "There are so many of them!"

"I'm afraid there's been a change of plans, zebra," Sir Trenton said, "but you're about to get scratched from tomorrow's race card."

Ruffshod and another brutish-looking horse sand-wiched Sandy on either side. She tried to escape, but they pushed her away, toward the Dalrymple barn.

Sir Trenton's eyes blazed as he glared at Stripes.

"Oh, don't you fret about her," he said. "As long as you don't race tomorrow, I wouldn't dream of harming her. *You*, on the other hand, need to be taught a lesson."

Before the zebra could say anything, Sir Trenton bellowed, "Show him!"

All at once, the other horses charged Stripes. They snorted and kicked and buffeted him with their huge bodies.

Stripes fought back, but he didn't stand a chance.

CHAPTER

Break for Freedom

"Cock-a-doodle-doo!" Reggie crowed the next morning. "Anyone seen Stripes?"

"He went out last night to find Sandy," Franny told Tucker.

"And you, Miss Softy, just let him go, didn't you?" the pony sighed. "Goose, we need you."

"I'm on it," the pelican replied. He stumbled forward a few awkward steps, then soared into the air.

A few minutes later, he began circling near the stream. "I found him!" Goose called. "Over here! Hey, kid! How many wings am I holding up?"

It didn't take long for the other animals to reach their friend. The zebra was badly bruised.

"I knew I should have stayed with him last night," Tucker sighed.

"Get him some water," Franny said.

Goose scooped some in his beak and gently splashed it onto the zebra. Stripes' eyes flickered open.

"They took Sandy," he said. "Sir Trenton's going to hurt her if I race."

"Those dirty rats!" Goose said. "I say we get busy and show those bums what for. Pow! Boom!"

"You're right," Franny said. "They've gone too far. Goose, let's rumble. It's time to kick some horse flank!"

Stripes tried to get up, but he was too weak.

"Just rest up here, kid," Tucker said. "We'll take care of business."

He and the other animals gathered outside the Walsh barn.

"Listen!" Tucker called. "If we don't rescue Sandy, Stripes can't race! We've got to break into the Dalrymple stables!"

Goose flapped his wings in excitement. "Now you're talking, baby! Let's do this — barnyard style!"

"Let's chloroform them from a crop duster!" Reggie added. "I've got nunchucks!" Everyone began talking all at once, calling out ideas.

"QUIET!" Franny bellowed. Everything went silent. "Now, listen," she continued. "To rescue Sandy, we all have to work *together*."

"Right," Reggie added. "So here's the plan. I don't know why I didn't think of this earlier! I could build a giant wooden chicken, and hide inside. Then, under cover of night, I'll jump out, and —" Everyone stared at him blankly. "Or I could just stay home," Reggie finished.

"Knock it off, Reggie!" said Tucker. "We need to rescue Sandy — there isn't much time!"

They all ran across the stream to the Dalrymple farm. They found a small spot in the fence to squeeze through — though it was a tight fit for Tucker — and headed for the lavish barn.

No humans were around, which was good, so the animals sneaked in. Unfortunately, Sir Trenton and Trenton's Pride stood between them and the rest of the stable. The animals hid in an unused stall.

"The family name is on the line today," they heard Sir Trenton telling his son. "If you don't win, don't bother showing your face in my stable again."

Trenton's Pride nodded, then headed off to find his trainer and rider.

"We've got to get Sir Trenton back in his stall," Franny whispered.

"Outta my way!" the pelican said. "This is a job for da Goose."

The bird took to the air and made a pass over the

big horse, dive-bombing him. Sir Trenton ducked, and Goose crashed into the wall behind him. An empty bucket toppled off a shelf and onto the pelican's head.

"Hey! Who killed the lights?" Goose sputtered.

Sir Trenton took aim with his big, metal-shod hooves, trying to crush the squawking pelican.

"So much for the featherhead," Tucker said. "What are we going to do now?"

"Say hello to 'Plan B'!" Buzz's tiny voice cried.

The two horseflies whizzed into the barn and circled Sir Trenton's head. Quick as a wink, Scuzz flew up Sir Trenton's nose.

"Whoa, dude, a little trim wouldn't kill ya!" Scuzz said, looking around inside the big thoroughbred's nostril.

Sir Trenton neighed, threw back his head, and sneezed. As he did, Goose fluttered out of his way. Scuzz shot out of the horse's nose and across the barn. "Grrrross!" he cried, crashing against the switch on the barn's stereo system. The music changed from soft classical to loud heavy metal.

Sir Trenton wheeled and bolted for his stall, trying to escape the blaring music. "Get back here, you chicken!" Goose called after him. "I'll fight you with one wing behind my back!" As soon as Sir Trenton was in his stall, Franny butted the door closed behind him. "Get Sandy," she called to Tucker.

The pony used his teeth to unlatch the gate on Sandy's stall. "Come on, let's go," he said. "Stripes needs you!"

Sir Trenton finally realized what was going on. But now he was trapped in his stall, and all he could do was call the other Dalrymple horses for help.

Sandy, Tucker, and the rest of the Walsh farm animals bolted out of the stable and headed for home.

Meanwhile, Stripes had gotten to his feet, and slowly plodded toward the fence that separated him from the Dalrymple property. He wanted to help Sandy, too.

Just then, Sandy, Tucker and the others hurried down the valley toward him. Tucker, Franny, and the rest squeezed through the gap. But Sandy stopped at the fence. She was too large to pass through. She looked frantically at Stripes. Behind her, Sir Trenton had escaped from his stall and was barreling toward them.

"Hurry!" Stripes said. "He's coming!"

Sandy paced back and forth near the small opening. "I won't fit!" she said.

"Then jump!" Stripes replied.

"I can't!" she said. "It's too high!"

"Yes you can," Stripes insisted. "I *know* you can. I believe in you."

Sir Trenton thundered closer, anger gleaming in his eyes. Sandy circled, took a few steps back, and then ran straight at the fence.

With the big horse right behind her, she jumped, sailing into the air. Her back legs cleared the fence as Sir Trenton snapped at her. The big horse pulled up, but it was too late. He crashed into the barrier.

"You can't do this to me!" he snarled at Stripes. "I am a *champion*! I am a legend! The affections of one filly do not make you a racehorse!"

"You're right," Stripes called back as he and the others made a beeline for home. "I'm *not* a racehorse. I'm a *zebra*! And I'm gonna race like nothing you've ever seen!" He turned to Tucker. "Come on, Tucker — let's go win ourselves a horse race."

Tucker smiled. "I like your attitude, kid," he said.

Everyone hurried back to the Walsh farm. Woodzie and the Walshes were waiting for them.

"Stripes, where have you been?" Channing cried. She looked half worried to death. "What's going on?"

Nolan didn't know what to make of all the activity, either, but he had a good guess. "I think it has something to do with the filly."

"It always does," Woodzie replied, laughing.

"Hey, she's from Philly?" Scuzz babbled. "I didn't know that! Oh, man, I love those Philly cheese steaks! Or any kind of cheese, really. Or steak. Or, actually, any kind of food from anywhere. Especially candy and poop. Uh, what were we talking about?"

Buzz sighed. "I hate my life."

"Let's get 'em loaded," Nolan told Channing.

"You got it, coach."

Nolan and Woodzie loaded Stripes and Tucker into the horse trailer.

"Just like the old days," Tucker said.

As the trailer pulled out of the driveway, the rest of the animals started toward the racetrack to root for their friend.

"Hey, wait for me! This chicken is flyin' the coop!" Reggie called as Sandy, Franny, Goose, and the horse-flies ran ahead without him.

⊔

Turfway Park buzzed with excitement. Colorful flags flapped in the wind. Stylish spectators filled the stands.

Clara Dalrymple stood on the infield, the center of attention — just the way she liked it. She smiled and checked her watch. She didn't want the media to know it, but she was secretly happy that the zebra hadn't showed up to race.

Trainers led the horses into the ring. The thoroughbreds, including Trenton's Pride and Ruffshod, pranced once around the track — both showing off and warming up.

Nolan's truck and horse trailer skidded into the parking lot. He, Channing, and Woodzie clambered out and raced to the tailgate. They let Tucker and Stripes out, and started preparing the zebra to race.

Nolan pulled a cardboard box off the front seat. He opened it and pulled out a colorful set of riding silks — much like the one Channing had been preparing for herself.

"These were your mom's," Nolan said to his daughter. "She would have wanted you to have them."

"Oh, Dad!" Channing replied, her eyes filling with tears. "I don't know what to say."

Nolan smiled at his daughter. "You were right, Channing. I've been too scared since Mom died. I kind of got stuck in a rut. I'm sorry. Can you forgive your old man?"

Channing threw her arms around him. "Dad," she said, "you're not old! Maybe a little gray around the edges, but that's it."

Nolan smiled again. "All right, we better hurry. Off with you."

Channing rushed to the dressing room to change. Nolan took Stripes to the saddling ring for final preparations. A few minutes later, Channing returned — looking every bit the professional jockey.

Nolan nodded to her. "Your mother would have been proud." He helped his daughter into the saddle and led Stripes through the dark tunnel leading to the track.

CHAPTER

Post Time

Nolan Walsh shared some final words of wisdom with his daughter as they walked through the tunnel. "It looks like Stripes had a tough night. If you think he's in any pain, pull back a little on the reins. He'll let you know if he wants to go on."

Channing nodded nervously at her dad. "Woodzie really thinks we have a chance, doesn't he?"

Nolan smiled. "He knows a good bet when he sees one."

"Yeah," Channing replied. "Stripes is the best."

Nolan looked proudly at his daughter. "I was talking about you."

Tucker walked alongside Stripes for one last pep talk.

"All right, kid, when you're in the starting gate," the pony said, "don't listen to the other racers. Let them do all the horsin' around. Save your energy for when it counts."

"I feel kinda sick to my stomach," Stripes said.

"Good," Tucker replied. "That means you're ready."

They arrived at the end of the tunnel. A thousand thoughts raced through Nolan's mind. There were so many things he wanted to say, but the time had come to let his little girl grow up. Nolan's eyes filled with tears as he took one last look at Channing. Then he took a deep breath and forced his hand to release the reins and let her go.

Tucker yelled after Stripes as he pulled away. "Go get 'em, kid."

As Tucker watched Stripes go, Sandy and Franny ran up behind him. Tucker did a double take, surprised to see them.

Franny smiled. "You didn't think we would let you have all the glory to yourself, did you?"

"Just like the old times, Franny," Tucker chuckled.

Fifty thousand people filled the grandstand — standing room only. Both zebra and rider felt very alone, despite the crowd.

Channing sensed that Stripes was even more nervous than she was. She hugged him around the neck and whispered in his ear, "No matter what happens, you'll always be my best boy."

The two of them made the slow circuit to the starting gate, surrounded by the big horses and riders. Clara Dalrymple spotted the zebra. Her jaw went tight and she nearly crushed the glass in her hand.

Nolan walked up next to her and smiled. "Hello, Clara. Beautiful day."

"It would be if you weren't ruining my race with that painted donkey," she replied.

"Your race?" Nolan asked. "Why is it your race? Because you spent the most money?"

"Well, frankly," Clara said, "*yes.*"

"I'll make you a deal," Nolan said. "If your horse wins, I'll sell you my farm. If my zebra wins, we get to keep your filly — the white jumper."

"Sandy?" Clara scoffed. "She's worth twice your land. Tell you what. You lose, you come back to work for me — a lifetime contract, in writing."

Nolan nodded. "Deal."

Clara smiled. "It'll be nice having you back, Nolan," she said.

The horseflies and the other animals made their way through the parking lot as Woodzie stepped up to the betting window. The old track rat checked the odds: 99 to 1. He smiled and laid down a big bet on the zebra to win.

The horses and Stripes approached the starting gate. Stripes' heart pounded in his chest.

"Didn't we tell you to stay away, freak?" Ruffshod growled.

"Are you crazy showing up here?" Trenton's Pride added. "Don't you know what my father will do?"

Despite the butterflies in his stomach, Stripes ignored them.

"Hey," Pride's jockey called to Channing, "you gonna set loose a lion behind that thing to make it run faster?" He laughed.

"Are those African drums I hear?" Ruffshod's jockey added.

Channing eyed the other jockeys coolly. "Where'd you two get your outfits," she asked. "from your wives' closets?" She turned forward and focused on the start of the race.

Near the rail, Tucker spoke to Goose, Buzz, and Scuzz. The three of them nodded and flew off, above the racetrack.

"The horses are all in," the track announcer said.

Suddenly, the bell sounded and the gate flew open.

The announcer's voice boomed above the field. "And . . . away they go!"

CHAPTER

Racing Stripes

Stripes shot out of the starting gate and immediately took the lead. The other horses thundered down the straightaway, just a few steps behind him.

The announcer's voice echoed above the sounds of pounding hooves. "Stripes is the quickest into stride, followed by Marietta's Rock, Johnny Rocket, and Sully's Secret. Trenton's Pride — the favorite — came out a step slow, and is currently seventh."

Stripes hugged the rail as the pack approached the first turn. Marietta's Rock passed him and took the lead as they rumbled around the curve. Ruffshod worked his way up past Sully's Secret and penned Stripes in.

The zebra looked for a way out, but Ruffshod had him trapped in the middle of the pack. And Ruffshod wouldn't budge.

Goose, flying lookout, saw Ruffshod's antics. He sent Buzz and Scuzz to inform Tucker. "Tell Tucker that Ruffshod's got him boxed in," Goose told them.

The flies responded with, "Copy that, Big Goose!" and relayed the pony's message back to Stripes.

"Tucker says to be patient," Buzz reported. "Stay where you are."

"Yeah," agreed Scuzz. "He said to hug the rail and make your move at the turn. You're doing great. Now let's fly! Hey, Buzz?" he added. "Did you ever notice the irony, when we say 'let's fly'?"

Buzz glanced over at him. "What are you talking about?"

"I'm just asking," Scuzz said. " 'Cuz we're flies and all, you know? "Let's fly"? Do you ever examine life and think about that stuff?"

"Would you shut up?!" Buzz exclaimed.

The flies darted out of the way as Ruffshod muscled in on the zebra once more. The big horse slammed into Stripes' flank. He pushed hard, trying to run the zebra into the rail.

Channing shot an angry look at Ruffshod's jockey; this kind of rough play was against the rules.

Stripes grunted as he took another shot to the ribs. Ruffshod smiled at him. "How does the rail taste, zebra?" the horse hissed. "You're out of your league!"

"They're cheating!" Buzz said to Scuzz. "That bully is hurting Stripes!"

"Not for long," Scuzz replied. He dove toward the big horse.

Stripes fought back, but it was all he could do to stay on his feet. With horses surrounding him on all sides, and Ruffshod playing dirty, he had no chance. At least not without some help.

Scuzz landed on Ruffshod's rear end and took a big bite.

Pain shot through Ruffshod's flanks. He neighed and nearly stumbled. Falling back in the pack, he reared, tossing his rider.

Scuzz circled back overhead. He spit out some of Ruffshod's fur and smiled. "That's why they call us *horse*flies," he said.

Buzz grinned. "You've always been a pain in the butt, and now it finally paid off."

"Oh! What a spill!" the announcer cried. "Ruffshod's out of the race, but his stablemate Trenton's Pride is moving like an absolute winner. He's right up there in the third spot! But sentimental choice Stripes is dropping back along the inside . . ."

Stripes now had the opening he had been waiting for, but his legs were starting to burn. Tucker had warned him about this, but Stripes had no idea how much it would hurt. Sensing Stripes' exhaustion, Channing pulled back on the reins.

"Had enough, boy?" Channing asked.

"They're rounding the clubhouse turn," the announcer said, "and Trenton's Pride is out in front, moving like a winner. He's been virtually unchallenged the whole way. The others are far back. Sentimental longshot Stripes is fading fast and now bringing up the rear."

Standing at the side of the track, Woodzie and Nolan hung their heads. Clara Dalrymple smiled triumphantly.

CHAPTER

Heart of a Champion

Buzz and Scuzz reported back to Tucker.

"The kid is wiped out," Buzz said.

"He's falling back quick," Scuzz agreed.

Tucker frowned and his ears drooped. "Tell him if he's hurting too much, he can ease up." The pony sighed. "Tell him . . . I understand."

The horseflies zipped around the track, bantering on the way.

"This is Superfly. We are proceeding to the target. Do you copy, Scuzz?" Buzz shouted.

"Hey!" Scuzz cried. "I told you to use my code name — 'Luke Scuzzwalker'!

Buzz replied, "I'm not gonna call you 'Luke Scuzzwalker'! Pick something more reasonable, like, uh . . . 'maggot'!" By this point, the flies had arrived at the zebra's ear.

"Kid," Buzz said, "coach says it's okay if you can't keep up. He understands."

The zebra set his jaw. "Tell Tucker I've got a message for him." He took a deep breath. *"Don't look back! Leave it all on the track!"*

When Tucker heard Stripes' message, he smiled and neighed, "BAH-WRONK!" It didn't sound exactly like the zebra's bray, but it was close enough.

Stripes spotted the finish line at the far end of the track. He kicked himself into high gear and almost shot out from underneath Channing. The world became a blur of motion around him. The other horses all seemed to be moving in slow motion — even Trenton's Pride at the head of the pack.

"Trenton's Pride is out there moving like a winner," the announcer's voice proclaimed. "At this point it's just a matter of how large the margin of victory will — but holy moly!" the announcer interrupted himself. "With an incredible burst of speed, Stripes the zebra is passing horses like they're standing still! He's flying! With a sixteenth of a mile to go, and Trenton's Pride is in the lead, here comes Stripes, charging along the inside! This race is not over yet!"

Stripes and Channing moved perfectly in sync, as if they'd been riding together all their lives.

The other horses fell away as Stripes raced forward. He passed them all. Only Trenton's Pride remained between him and the finish. The two of them rocketed toward the line, dueling for the win.

Nolan and Woodzie cheered so loud they almost lost their voices. "Come on, Channing, get into him!" Woodzie shouted. "GO! GO! GO!" Nolan screamed.

Buzz and Scuzz sat on Woodzie's hat and pumped their little arms back and forth, as if they were the jockey riding Stripes.

Stripes pulled up behind Trenton's Pride, practically nipping at his tail. Channing gave him a gentle tap and the zebra knew what to do.

He cut inside and shot along the gap near the rail. Trenton's Pride looked astonished as the zebra pulled up next to him.

"They're nearing the finish line!" the announcer blared. "These two are now locked together! They're absolutely neck and neck, but Stripes is all heart! He won't give an inch."

Stripes nosed forward, and — for an instant — had the lead.

Pride responded, surging ahead and taking it right back.

Stripes gave it everything he had and caught up once again.

"It's Trenton's Pride!" the announcer said. "Now it's Stripes! Trenton's Pride! Stripes! Trenton's Pride!"

Stripes didn't dare even glance sideways. He looked straight ahead and pushed for the finish line. Sweat poured down his body. Every muscle in him ached. His ears rang with Tucker's words: "Leave it all on the track!"

The horse and the zebra thundered over the finish line, neck and neck.

The announcer's voice blared over the roar of the crowd. . . .

CHAPTER

The Winner

"Stripes has won by a nose!" the announcer cheered. "The zebra has won the Kentucky Open, narrowly beating Trenton's Pride in a driving finish!"

Woodzie let out a whoop so loud that it nearly knocked Buzz and Scuzz off the brim of his hat.

The crowd gasped and cheered — a combination of joy and disbelief.

The Walsh animals neighed, and brayed, and crowed with delight. Buzz and Scuzz high-fived each other.

Stripes slowed to a walk, panting heavily. Channing eased up on the reins and hugged him around the neck. "That's my best boy!" she said.

As Stripes turned toward the Winner's Circle, he couldn't quite believe it. *I won. I can't believe it — I won!* he thought. Just then, Trenton's Pride trotted up alongside him.

"I don't care what my father says," Trenton's Pride admitted, "you *are* a racer. A great one."

Stripes nodded. "Back at you," he said.

Nolan Walsh ducked under the rail and sprinted out to his daughter. Channing hopped off Stripes and ran into her father's arms.

"Did you see him?" she said. "Did you see him, Dad? He almost shot out from under me."

"Your mom would be so proud," Nolan said. "And so am I."

Finally, the official results, in order of finish, lit up the board: (12) (1) (9) (5).

Clara Dalrymple stormed past the Winner's Circle. "I want an inquiry! That zebra was all over the track! I want him disqualified!"

Goose circled over her head. "I hope you like this as much as I did when I ate it," he said. And with that, he dropped a load right on the top of Clara's head. SPLAT!

"Nice shot," Tucker said to Franny. "Maybe he really is a hit bird!"

Goose landed on the ground next to them, clearly pleased with himself.

"Great job, Goose," Tucker said. "You make a lousy gangster, but you're a stand-up pelican."

Goose was shocked for a minute. "Hey! That's the nicest thing a very short horse has ever said to me."

Off to the side, Woodzie counted his money. It looked to be enough to choke a horse.

Channing and Stripes strode proudly into the Winner's Circle. Nolan gave his daughter a leg up, onto the zebra's back. Each looked even more proud than the other.

Reporters snapped pictures at a mile a minute. A swarm of TV cameras hovered around the trio.

Woodzie, his pockets bulging with cash, pushed his way through the crowd. "Clear the way," he called, "rich winner coming through!"

Woodzie stood side by side with Stripes and the Walshes as the race officials put a wreath of roses around Stripes' neck. Nolan held the zebra's reins in one hand and a big silver trophy in the other. Channing grinned from ear to ear, looking very much like her mother in the portraits on the barn wall.

Sandy raced to the side of the track, carrying an exhausted Reggie on her back. It had taken him a lot longer to run to the track than it had taken Tucker and the rest. "Has the race started yet? Did I miss anything? I thought you guys were gonna wait for me!" the rooster crowed.

All the other Walsh farm animals pushed through the rail to join Stripes — Sandy, Franny, Goose, Reggie, and even the horseflies.

"It's okay," Nolan told the race officials as Sandy approached. "That horse belongs to *me*. They *all* belong to me."

The paddock boss shook his head. "That's a nice . . . collection you've got there." He smiled.

Stripes looked around for Tucker. Seeing the pony in his usual modest spot behind all the action, the zebra left the ring to get him.

"Get back there!" Tucker said to him. "You belong in the Winner's Circle."

"Not unless you come too," Stripes said. "I'd be nothing without you."

Stripes nudged the pony and, reluctantly, Tucker entered the circle and stood in the front, right next to Stripes.

Just as the photographer snapped the official winner's picture, Stripes leaned forward and dropped his winning wreath around Tucker's neck.

"You know," Franny called out to Tucker, "those

roses make you look like Elvis. Very Elvis." For once, Tucker didn't mind the teasing.

He blinked back a tear. "Thanks, kid," he whispered to Stripes.

Channing and Nolan put their arms around their barnyard family and gave them all a hug. The photographers took countless pictures that would soon appear in newspapers and magazines around the world.

None of them — not the farmer, nor his daughter, nor the pony, nor the zebra who had just become "the best of the best" — had ever been happier.